My Leafs Sweater

My Leafs Sweater

by Mike Leonetti
illustrations by Sean Thompson

RAINCOAST BOOKS
Vancouver

First published in 1998 by

Raincoast Books
9050 Shaughnessy Street
Vancouver, B.C.
V6P 6E5
(604) 323-7100

www.raincoast.com

4 5 6 7 8 9 10

CANADIAN CATALOGUING IN PUBLICATION DATA

Leonetti, Mike, 1958-
My Leafs sweater

ISBN 1-55192-194-4 (HBK) 1-55192-306-8 (PBK)

1. Toronto Maple Leafs (Hockey team) – Juvenile fiction. 2. Hockey – Juvenile fiction. I. Thompson, Sean, 1966- II. Title.

PS8573.E58734M92 1998 JC813'.54 C98-910410-9
PZ7.L55My 1998

The Canada Council for the arts since 1957 | Le Conseil des Arts du Canada depuis 1957

Raincoast Books gratefully acknowledges the support of the Government of Canada, through the Book Publishing Industry Development Program, the Canada Council for the Arts and the Department of Canadian Heritage. We also acknowledge the assistance of the Province of British Columbia, through the British Columbia Arts Council.

ACKNOWLEDGEMENTS

The writer would like to thank Maria Leonetti and Nick Pitt for all their help with the original story; thanks to Mark Stanton and Brian Scrivener at Raincoast Books for believing in this idea and Stephen Eaton Hume for helping it along its way; and to Sean Thompson, whose paintings brought this concept to life. ***Hommage à Roch Carrier.***

PRINTED AND BOUND IN SINGAPORE

To my first born child and to all children who grow up wanting to wear the Maple Leafs sweater.
– ML

To Rachelle, for her love and patience, and to my folks, for all the support, pencils and paper.
– ST

It was a snowy Saturday night. The wind was howling. I was happy to be inside because *Hockey Night in Canada* was about to start. This show made every Saturday night in the winter very special.
I never missed it.

The team I cheered for was the Toronto Maple LEafs, and my favourite player was their captain, Darryl Sittler. He wore a white sweater with a big blue maple leaf on the chest and number 27 on the back. I liked Darryl because he always tried his best. You could see it every time he was on the ice.

I wanted to be just like Darryl Sittler, and I wanted a Maple Leafs sweater just like his.

GO
LEAFS
GO!

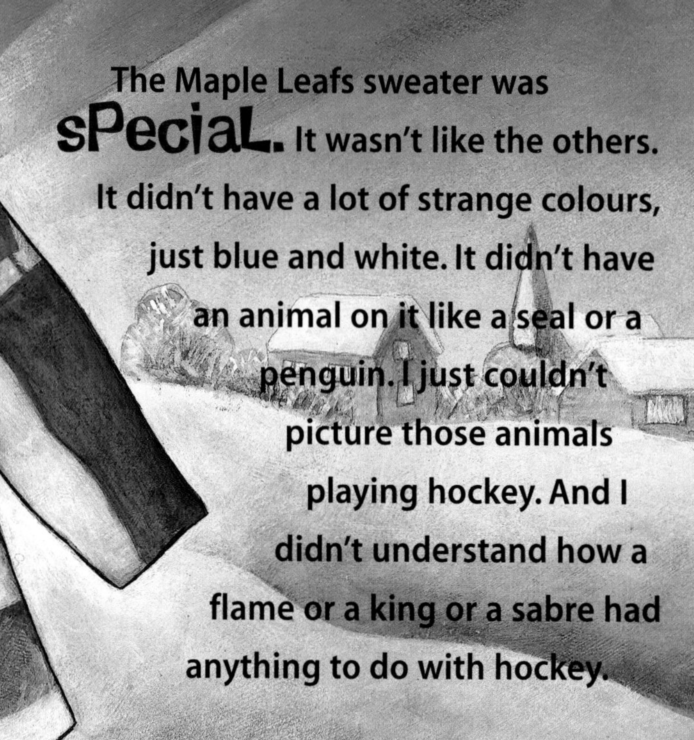

The Maple Leafs sweater was special. It wasn't like the others. It didn't have a lot of strange colours, just blue and white. It didn't have an animal on it like a seal or a penguin. I just couldn't picture those animals playing hockey. And I didn't understand how a flame or a king or a sabre had anything to do with hockey.

But I'd seen maple leaves with my own eyes, frozen in the ice below my skates, trapped there until spring. They had something to do with skating and seeing your breath on a cold day. Maple leaves turning colour meant the start of the hockey season, a sign that winter was coming.

The maple leaf on the sweater stood out because it was simple and true, just like the leaves on the tree in front of our house. I could also see a big red maple leaf in the middle of the Canadian flag out in front of my school. It meant something to everybody, even to the people who were new to this country.

Best Wishes,
Darryl Sittler
TORONTO
MAPLE
LEAFS
GO
LEAFS
GO!

I had a poster of Darryl Sittler and an autographed photo of him on my bedroom wall. I knew how many goals he had scored and how many points and assists he had. I had a collection of all his hockey cards since he began playing for the Leafs. I had a hockey stick like his, and I even taped it the way he did.

All my friends had a favourite player they pretended to be, but whenever we played hockey I was always the first to call out, "I'm SittlEr!"

Next Saturday was my birthday, so the next day I decided to ask my Mom and Dad about my pResent.

"Mom, do you think I could get a Leafs sweater for my birthday?"

"I don't know, Michael. Those are expensive sweaters."
I stood in silence. I wanted that sweater more than anything else in the world.

"I have an idea," my Dad said. "What if you save some money? You could help your mother with things around the…"

"WAit!" I exclaimed. "I have saved money – from my allowance!"

Surprised, my Dad looked at me. "How much?"

"I have five dOllars!"

My Mom and Dad smiled at each other.

"Well," he said, "since you've saved some money yourself, then maybe we can think about it."

I turned to my Mom. "Is it oKay then, Mom?"

"If you're a good boy and do your school work, we'll get you a Maple Leafs sweater on your birthday," she said.

I was so happy I could hardly stand still!

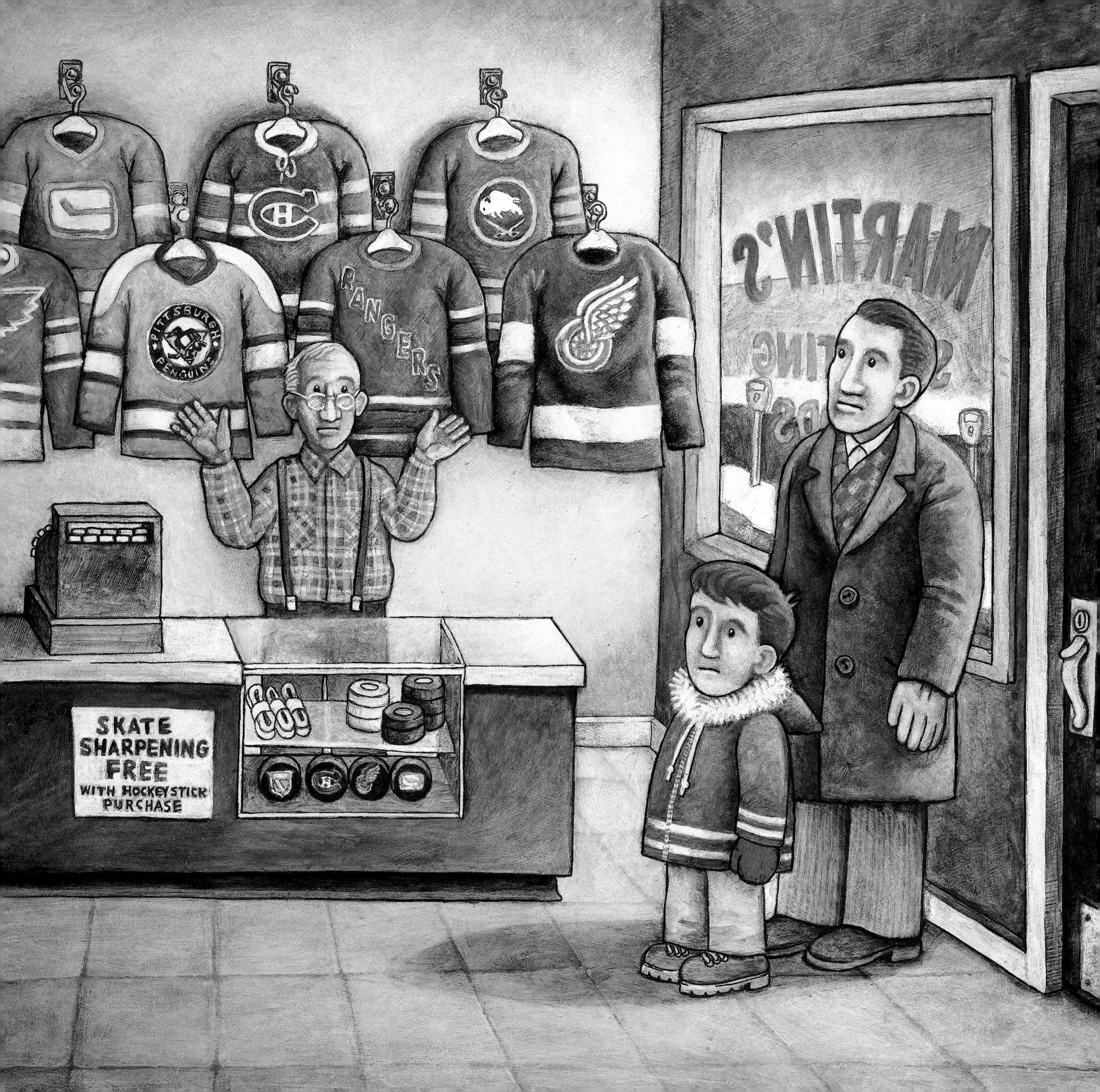
MARTIN'S
PITTSBURGH PENGUINS
RANGERS
SKATE SHARPENING FREE WITH HOCKEYSTICK PURCHASE

I spent the next week trying very hard to be good. When Saturday morning came my Dad and I got in the car and drove down to Martin's Sports on Main Street. They had a lot of hockey sweaters. Canadiens. Red Wings. Rangers. Sabres. Penguins. But not a single Maple Leafs.

My Dad went up to Mr. Martin. "Sorry," he said. "Sold the last one an hour ago. Why don't you try the mall down the road?"

SOLD OUT? How could that be?

We drove to the mall. Being Saturday, it was busy, and it took us a while to find a parking space. We had to walk from the farthest corner of the lot, then down the length of the mall to a sporting goods store. They had plenty of sweaters, too. Blackhawks. Bruins. Flames. Flyers. Kings.
But no Maple Leafs.

"Sold out," the storekeeper said. He held up a Canadiens sweater. "What about this one?"

I could see there was going to be a problem. Either you loved the Leafs or you didn't understand.

I folded my arms and looked away. "No," I said.
"It's not the same."

As we left the store the salesman said, "Have you tried the store at Maple Leaf Gardens?"

Dad and I looked at each other. **Why nOt!**

"C'mon!" Dad said. We jumped in the car and just kept going. When we finally stopped outside Maple Leaf Gardens, I ran into the store ahead of Dad.

But all the sweaters they had were way too large.

Now I was reAlly sad, and I wanted to cry.

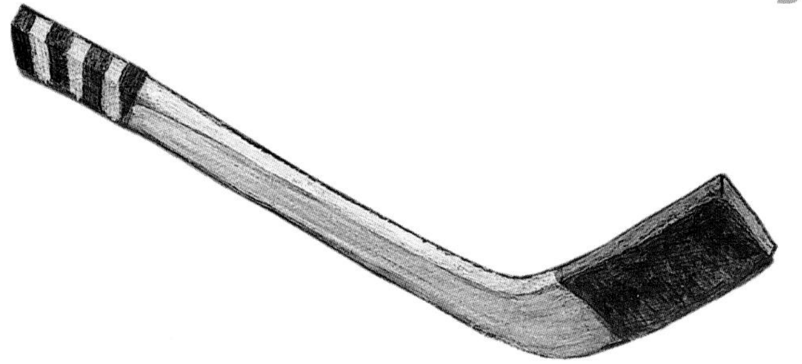

TORONTO MAPLE LEAFS
TORONTO MAPLE LEAFS
TORONTO MAPLE LEAFS
C
27
21
MAPLE
GARDENS SHOP

TONIGHT NHL HOCKEY
TORONTO
VS BOSTON
MAPLE

As we were leaving the building I noticed a sign outside the main door: TONIGHT NHL HOCKEY: TORONTO vs BOSTON. The Bruins had been on a winning streak and were a good team. It should be a great game. I asked my Dad if we could buy tickets. He said he'd try, but he reminded me not to get my hopes up because these games were usually sold out well in advance.

Dad walked up to the man behind the window and they spoke for a few minutes. I closed my eyes and prayed there would be two tickets. I saw Dad reach for his wallet. Yes! I must have jumped five feet in the air.

"We were lucky. Someone who couldn't go tonight turned their tickets in just a few minutes ago," Dad explained.

We called Mom and told her we wouldn't be home until late. As soon as the ticket takers were ready, my Dad and I passed through the turnstile. I was now going to see the Leafs in person for the very first time!

Dad pointed to the pictures on the wall in the main lobby and read the names to me. He stopped at the photo of Dave Keon and said he was his favourite player when he was a boy. We also stopped at the pictures of Syl Apps, Ted Kennedy and George Armstrong. I didn't know any of these players, but Dad said they had been captains of the Leafs, just like Darryl Sittler.

He also pointed out the photo of Frank Mahovlich. Dad said he wore number 27 before Darryl did. He showed me how the maple leaf on the sweaters had changed over the years. I could tell Dad was enjoying telling me about all this.

Dad bought me a souvenir program with a picture of Darryl on the cover and we stopped and bought hot dogs and a soda pop. Then we went up the stairs to our seats.

SYL APPS
TED KENN
GEORGE ARM
DAVE KEON
FRANK MAHOVLICH
MAPLE LEAF
MAGAZINE

TORONTO
VISITOR
TORONTO
THOMAS
30
TURNBULL
2
22

The ice surface was so much bigger than the rink I played on at home, and all the lines were freshly painted. A booming voice came out of the loudspeakers and told us who the referee would be and who would play in goal for each team.

The crowd let out a cHeer as the Maple Leafs skated onto the ice to start the game.

I couldn't believe it: a little while ago I was disappointed because I didn't have a Leafs sweater, and now I was watching my hero in person!

Before I knew what was happening, Darryl had set up two goals with lightning-quick passes to teammates.

Then, early in the second period, he swatted the puck right out of mid-air into the Boston net. A little later he stepped over the blue line and slapped the puck past the Bruins goalie. Then he took a pass and one-timed a shot for his third goal. A hat trick in one period! And he also picked up two more assists.

Then, in the first minute of the third period, Darryl took a pass in full stride, swept around a Boston defenceman and put a wrist shot into the far corner of the net for his fourth goal! But my hero wasn't done yet. Darryl came back down the ice and kept the puck away from the Bruin defencemen before blazing a shot into the far side of the net. Five goals! Everyone at Maple Leaf Gardens rose to their feet and gave Darryl a standing ovation. His teammates were mobbing him on the ice.

I was jumping up and down in my seat. Dad was screaming, "Pass it to Sittler! PaSs it to SittlEr!"

Just when I thought it couldn't get any better, Darryl scored his sixth goal of the game. He was trying to complete a pass to a teammate from behind the Boston net when the puck hit a Bruin defenceman on the skate and went through the goalie's legs!

That night Sittler did something no other player in the history of hockey had ever done, scoring six goals and four assists in one game. My throat was so hoarse from yelling that I could hardly talk, but I still cheered Darryl when he was named as the first star at the end of the game. The Leafs won 11 to 4, and it was my beSt birthday ever!

The next day I grabbed my stick and skates and rAn all the way to the rink. I didn't have a new sweater, but that was all right. Maybe next Christmas I would ask for one. I had just seen my hero star in one of the best hockey games ever played. That was better than any sweater.

As I skated along the ice with my friends, I looked down and saw red maple leaves frozen in the ice, and I remembered what hockey was all about. I scored two goals in the game and our team won. Afterwards my friends slapped me on the back and said, "Nice game, SittLer."

4
16
35

GO LEAFS GO!
TORONT
MAPLE
LEAFS
MAPLE LEAF
MAGAZINE

That night I dreamed about one day playing for the Leafs in Maple Leaf Gardens. I could hear the announcer say, "Here comes number 27 straight up the ice! He dekes around two defencemen and moves in on the goalie! He sHoots! He scOres!"

One day, maybe my dream will come true.

Darryl Sittler

Darryl Sittler's NHL record 10-point game took place on February 7, 1976, in an 11-4 victory over the Boston Bruins at Maple Leaf Gardens. He also scored five goals in one playoff game against the Philadelphia Flyers on April 22, 1976, tying an NHL record. He was a respected captain of the Leafs and still holds many team records, including most career hat tricks (18), most career goals (389) and most career points (916). He was honoured by being elected to the Hockey Hall of Fame in 1989. Darryl firmly believes in having fun while playing the game and that a high level of sportsmanship is an important part of hockey. He also emphasizes the importance of education and of staying in school.

Darryl shared his love of hockey with his father, Ken, who told Darryl as a young boy that, if he practised hard and dedicated himself to improving every day, he might make it to the NHL and play at Maple Leaf Gardens, just like the players Darryl and his Dad used to watch on *Hockey Night in Canada*.